KAMISHIBAI MAN

written and illustrated by

ALLEN SAY

Houghton Mifflin Company Boston 2005

Walter Lorraine Books

For Margaret Eisenstadt, Donna Tamaki, and Tara McGowan

Walter Lorraine 〔wℛ〕 Books

www.houghtonmifflinbooks.com

Library of Congress Cataloging-in-Publication Data

Say, Allen.
  Kamishibai man / Allen Say.
      p. cm.
  "Walter Lorraine books."
  Summary: After many years of retirement, an old Kamishibai man—a Japanese street performer
who tells stories and sells candies—decides to make his rounds once more even though such
entertainment declined after the advent of television.
  ISBN-13: 978-0-618-47954-2
  ISBN-10: 0-618-47954-6
[1. Kamishibai—Fiction. 2. Street theater—Fiction. 3. Storytelling—Fiction.4. Japan—Fiction.]
I. Title.
  PZ7.S2744Kam 2005
  [Fic]—dc22
                                                                    2005006319

Printed in the United States of America
WOZ 10 9 8 7 6 5 4 3 2 1

FOREWORD

When I think of my childhood in Japan, I think of kamishibai. It means "paper theater." Every afternoon, the kamishibai man came on a bicycle that had a big wooden box mounted on the back seat. The box had drawers full of candies and a stage at the top. We bought candies and listened to the man's stories.

As he told the stories, the kamishibai man would slide out the picture cards in the stage one by one and put them in the back, like shuffling a deck of cards. The stories were actually one never-ending tale, with each installment ending with the hero or heroine hanging from a cliff or getting pushed off it.

"To be continued," the kamishibai man would say with a grin, and we children would groan, but not too much. Tomorrow the hero and heroine would be saved for new adventures, and we would have our candies.

Yes, they were cliffhangers. So when I came to America, that was one expression that nobody had to explain to me. Today, any sort of cliffhanger reminds me of the happy memories that kamishibai had given me. And with this book, though it has no high cliffs, let me be your "paper theater man" for a day. You'll have to get your own sweets.

Allen Say

Not so long ago in Japan, in a small house on a hillside, there lived an old man and his wife. Even though they never had children of their own, they called each other "Jiichan" and "Baachan." Jiichan is Grandpa, and Baachan is Grandma.

One day, Baachan said, "Jiichan, you haven't said a word in three days."

"Umm, I've been thinking how much I miss going on my rounds," he said.

Baachan stared. "How many years has it been?" she asked.

"Umm, yes, quite a while . . . but my legs are good. And I've kept the bicycle in good order."

". . . I don't know. But one day won't hurt, I suppose. Should I make some candies?"

"That would be very nice," Jiichan said.

The next day, Jiichan rode his bicycle down the hillside in the first light of morning.

"Umm, how many years has it been?" he asked himself. "And do I remember such a fine morning? All so fresh and young . . . Well, good morning to you, rickety old bridge, still going strong after all these years, um, mmm." He began to hum a tune that his mother used to sing when he was a small boy.

When he came to the city, he stopped humming.

"This isn't right," he said. "I must have taken a wrong turn . . . but there's that old house I used to go by every afternoon . . ."

A car horn blasted at him, then another.

"Why are there so many cars all of a sudden? Look at these tall buildings! You'd think I was in another country!"

A truck blasted its horn behind him.

He pulled into a vacant lot and panted. "Can't a man ride his bicycle in peace? Don't remember such rude drivers." Catching his breath, he looked across the street and gaped.

"Can this be? There's that old noodle shop . . . used to be the only building here . . . that and a nice park all around. Now look at all these shops and restaurants. They chopped down all those beautiful trees for them. Who needs to buy so many things and eat so many different foods?"

Shaking his head, he slowly took the canvas off the box on his bicycle. He propped up the stage and checked the story cards inside, patting each painting. Then he opened the bottom drawer in the box.

"Umm, you little jewels," he said, and started to hum again. "Thank you, Baachan—you make good candies, just like in the old days."

From the top drawer he took out two wooden blocks, and
holding one in each hand he hit them together. A sharp, loud clack
rang out.

"Come gather around me, little ones, your kamishibai man is
here again!"

Clack, clack!

"Come get your sweets and listen to my stories!"

Clack, clack, clack!

"Ah, yes, I can see you now, all your bright faces, clasping coins in your little hands, so happy to hear my clappers, so happy to see your kamishibai man!

"Patience, everyone! You'll get your sweets, each and every
one of you; I have all your favorites—red ones and green ones
and the soft ones on sticks. And here comes that boy, the one who
never has any money . . . umm, I'll get to him later.

"So, which story will it be today? The mighty 'Peach Boy'! Born from a giant peach! But wait, let's start at the beginning, umm . . . Long, long ago, there once lived an old man and his wife who had no children . . .

"After 'The Peach Boy,' 'The Bamboo Princess' was a nice change, a gentle story. Then my favorite, 'The Old Man Who Made Cherry Trees Bloom.' And when I was finished, you all went home happy, except for that poor boy. 'Would you like a candy?' I asked once. He said, 'I don't like candies!' and ran away.

"Then one night I was going home and saw a crowd of people gathered in front of a shop. They were staring at something called television. I was curious too, but not for long. It showed moving pictures; they were all jerky and blurry and had no colors at all.

"It wasn't long after that when television antennas started to sprout from the rooftops like weeds in the springtime. And the more they grew, the fewer boys and girls came out to listen to my stories.

"How can they like those blurry pictures better than my beautiful paintings? I asked. But there was nothing to be done. As I went around the familiar neighborhoods, the children started to act as though they didn't know me anymore.

"Even so, I went on clacking my clappers, and one day a little girl poked her head out the window and shushed me. Imagine, a little girl shushing me. The kamishibai man was making too much noise!

"I sat on a park bench and ate a candy for lunch. How could the world change so quickly? Was I a bad storyteller? Then that boy came, the boy who didn't like candies. 'Why aren't you watching television?' I asked. 'I don't like television!' he said. 'But you like my stories,' I said, and he nodded his little head.

"I got up and set the stage. 'What's your favorite story?' I asked. '"Little One Inch,"' he answered. So I told him the story of a brave little boy who was only one inch tall. And as I told the story, the boy never looked at the picture cards in the stage. He was looking at me the whole time, with his mouth wide open. He even smiled now and then.

"When I finished the story, I started to take out some sweets to give him, but he was already running away. 'Wait!' I shouted, but he kept running and never turned his head. That was the last time I saw that boy. That was the last day I was a kamishibai man . . ."

"I was that boy!" a loud voice cried out.

Startled, the kamishibai man looked up and saw that a large crowd had gathered before him.

"We grew up with your stories!" someone else shouted.

"Tell us 'Little One Inch' again!"

"And 'The Bamboo Princess'!"

"'The Peach Boy'!"

He started to say something, and people began to clap their hands. He took a deep bow, and the applause got louder.

A young man with a movie camera struggled up to him. They bowed to each other, and as the old man gave him a candy, a roar went up.

"Look, he has all the same old sweets!"

"Just like the old days!"

And the office clerks and shopkeepers, bankers and waitresses, housewives and deliverymen, all lined up in a big circle around the kamishibai man.

It was dark when he got home. Baachan was watching the evening news. The kamishibai man was the featured story.

"I see you had a busy day," she said.

"It was a good day." Jiichan nodded.

"Will you be going out tomorrow?"

"Umm, yes. And the day after."

"Then you need more sweets."

"That would be very nice. Umm, could you make it twice the usual amount?"

"I'll see if I have enough sugar," she said, and shut the television off.

AFTERWORD

Kamishibai (kah-mee-she-bye) is said to have started in the 1930s, but it is part of a long tradition of picture storytelling in Japan. Early precursors of kamishibai were not easily transportable, but in the late 1920s a form of kamishibai was developed for a small wooden stage that could be strapped onto a bicycle and carried from town to town. The kamishibai performer made a living by selling candy, and he told his stories in serial fashion so that audiences came repeatedly to buy candy and to hear the next episode of the story. Just as precursors of kamishibai had modeled themselves on popular forms of traditional theater, such as kabuki, this new form drew heavily on techniques and story lines from popular films. Many of the performers had worked as *benshi* (narrators for silent films), and, when talking pictures came into Japan, they turned to kamishibai for their livelihood.

Kamishibai is poor man's theater, and it flourished during a time when Japan experienced extreme financial hardship. In the 1930s, Japan suffered an economic depression that sent many people onto the streets looking for a way to live from one day to the next, and kamishibai offered artists and storytellers a meager living. During and after World War II, kamishibai became an ever more integral part of the society as a form of entertainment that could be transported into bomb shelters and even devastated neighborhoods. At this time, it was entertainment as much for adults as for children.

By the 1950s and the advent of television, kamishibai had become so popular that television was initially referred to as *denki* (electric) *kamishibai.* As Japan became increasingly affluent, however, kamishibai became associated with poverty and backwardness. The kamishibai teller's candy was considered unsanitary and the stories unwholesome. Increasingly parents and educators pushed to have kamishibai stories harnessed to educational aims, and today the kamishibai storyboards published in Japan are mainly sold to schools and libraries. Eventually kamishibai as a street-performance art all but disappeared. The artists who had made their living with kamishibai turned to more lucrative pursuits, notably the creation of *manga* (comic books) and later *anime,* but they never forgot their roots in kamishibai.

—Tara McGowan,
Japanese folklore scholar